Megamouths and Hammerheads

Written by Jo Windsor

In this book
you will
see sharks.

You will see...

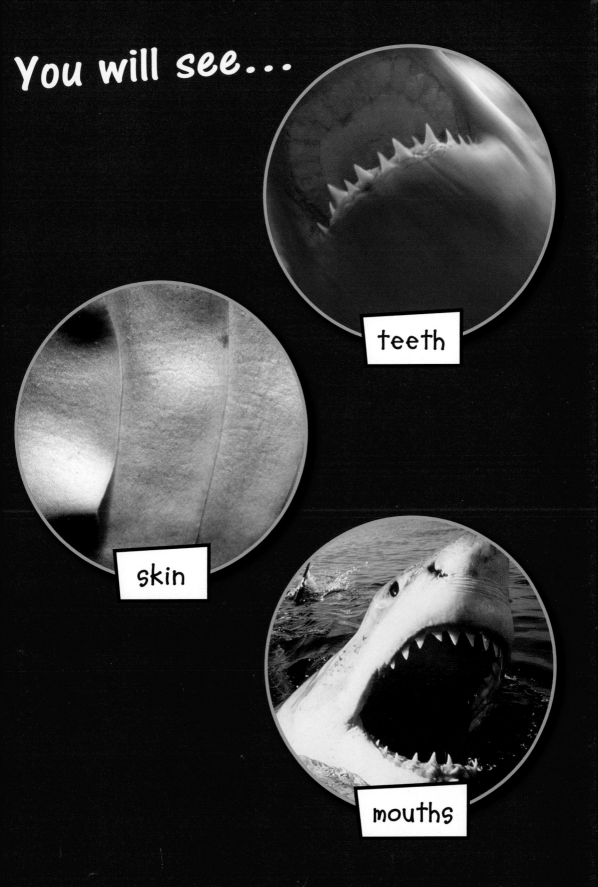

teeth

skin

mouths

Sharks come in all sizes and shapes.

Some are big.
Some are little.

Some have big mouths.
Some have big heads.
Some have long noses.

This shark likes to live
down at the bottom of the sea.

It can hide in the sand.

The shark stays at
the bottom to...

sleep   Yes? No?

hide from
danger   Yes? No?

get food   Yes? No?

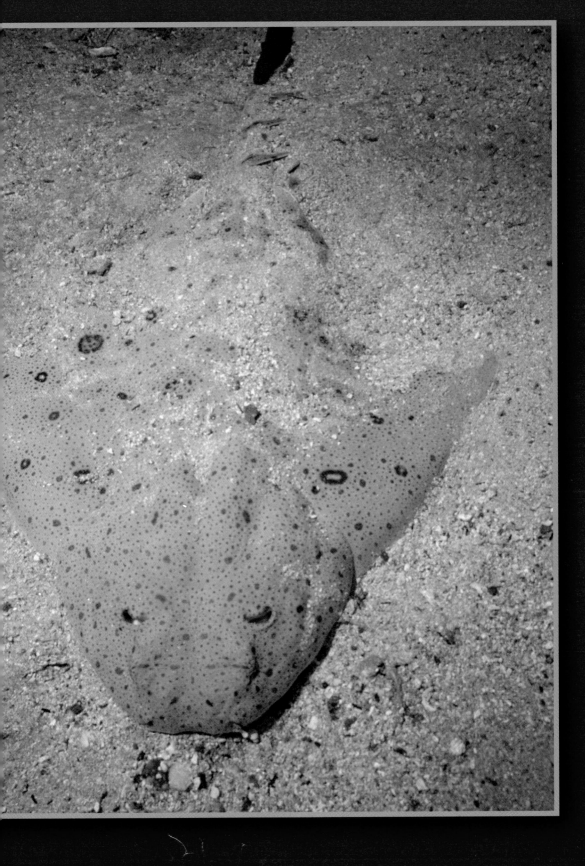

Look at the skin.
Shark's skin!

This shark swims fast.
Its skin helps it go fast.
Look at its tail and fins.

The shark swims fast to...

win a race   Yes? No?

get food   Yes? No?

get away
from danger   Yes? No?

shark's skin

tail

fins

Look at this head!

This shark is big.
It has a very big head.

Look at its eyes.
They are on the side of its head.

This shark makes its head
go from side to side
to find its food.

This is a big, big shark.
It lives deep down in the water.
Look at its mouth!

It has a big, big mouth,
but it eats little animals and
plants for its food.

All sharks eat little
animals and plants. Yes? No?

This is the biggest shark.

This shark has a big mouth.
It eats little animals
and plants, too.

Divers like to swim
with this shark.
This shark will swim up
to see who the divers are.

Look at the teeth!
These teeth are very sharp.

Some sharks have lots and lots of teeth.
Sharks that have teeth like this
like to eat big animals.

Sharks have...

teeth   Yes? No?

feathers   Yes? No?

fins   Yes? No?

Look at this!
Shark food!

Some sharks get
their food at night.
Some sharks get
their food in the day.

All sharks
eat meat.   Yes? No?

Some sharks lay eggs,
and some sharks have live babies.

Baby sharks are called pups.
Pups can take care of themselves.

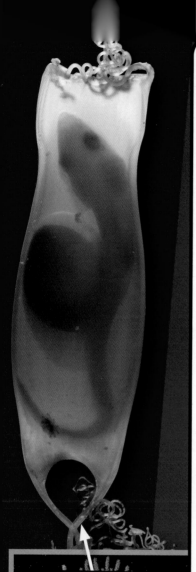

shark egg

Index

A yes/no chart

The biggest shark
lives deep in the water. Yes? No?

A shark's skin
helps it swim fast. Yes? No?

Some sharks lay eggs. Yes? No?

Sharks eat plants. Yes? No?

Some sharks like
to eat meat. Yes? No?

All sharks are big. Yes? No?

Sharks have
sharp teeth. Yes? No?

Some sharks
have babies. Yes? No?

Word Bank

diver

nose

eye

plant

fin

tail

head

teeth